The Lucky Boots

A Tale about Learning from Mistakes

Retold by Jacqueline A. Ball
Illustrated by Renate Lohmann

Famous Fables

Reader's Digest Young Families

Once upon a time, a professor named Dr. Knapp attended a dinner party at the elegant home of an army captain in Copenhagen. As he was leaving, Dr. Knapp stopped to admire a large painting of a knight.

"Imagine living back then," Dr. Knapp said. "I wish we could go back to those exciting times!"

In the cloak room, two fairies listened. One was a fairy-in-training named Lucky. The other was her teacher, a fairy named Careful.

"Now's my chance!" exclaimed Lucky. She pushed a pair of boots in front of the others.

"What are you doing?" Careful asked with concern.

"These are lucky boots just for tonight," the little fairy explained. "I sprinkled them with fairy dust for my test!"

All fairies had to pass a magic test to earn their permanent wings.

"If that gentleman makes a wish while wearing these boots," Lucky continued, "his wish will come true—and I'll get my wings!"

"But he didn't make a real wish," Careful said. "What we heard was wishful thinking. That's not the same as wishing for something you really, really want."

Lucky wasn't listening. She was watching Dr. Knapp slip on the lucky boots over his shoes, mistaking them for his own.

Once outside, Dr. Knapp walked by the river.
He was still dreaming about the dashing days of the
knights. "If only I could go back to that time," he wished.

Suddenly Dr. Knapp's feet sank into mud. Thick
fog swirled around. He heard drums close by.

"Halt!" a gruff voice shouted.

Dr. Knapp was surrounded by knights! They were
dressed like the knight in the painting. But these knights
were pointing their sharp weapons at him!

"We're looking for the person who stole a stack of gold pieces from the king's castle," the biggest knight said. He peered closely at the professor's face. "Someone who looks just like you! Why are you hiding in those strange clothes?" the knight demanded.

"I-I-I didn't steal anything. I don't know the king or where his castle is. You're making a t-t-terrible mistake!" stammered Dr. Knapp.

"We'll see about that," said the knight. He grabbed Dr. Knapp and turned him upside down, shaking him by the boots.

"Stop!" cried Dr. Knapp just as the boots came off. Dr. Knapp tumbled down to the ground. Magically, he returned to the time and place he had left. He was unharmed. The boots landed near a watchman, asleep on a bench.

Dr. Knapp rubbed his eyes and looked around. "I must have been daydreaming. Who would want to live among such ruffians!" And then Dr. Knapp went home.

"See what I mean about wishful thinking?" asked Careful. "These magic boots can cause a lot of trouble!"

Lucky frowned. "Maybe the boots will work better this time!" she said, pointing to the bench.

The watchman had awakened from his nap. He looked at the boots. He looked at the holes in the bottoms of his shoes. Then he pulled on the boots.

"I wish I could sleep all night long, like a baby," he said aloud.

Instantly the watchman turned into a sleeping baby!

At that moment, a young woman walked by. She saw the huge sleeping baby dressed like a watchman and sprang back.

"Oh, dear!" she exclaimed.

Just then, the captain walked up. He was bringing the watchman a late-night snack.

"Oh, dear!" he exclaimed when he saw the baby.

The giant baby's snores echoed in the night.

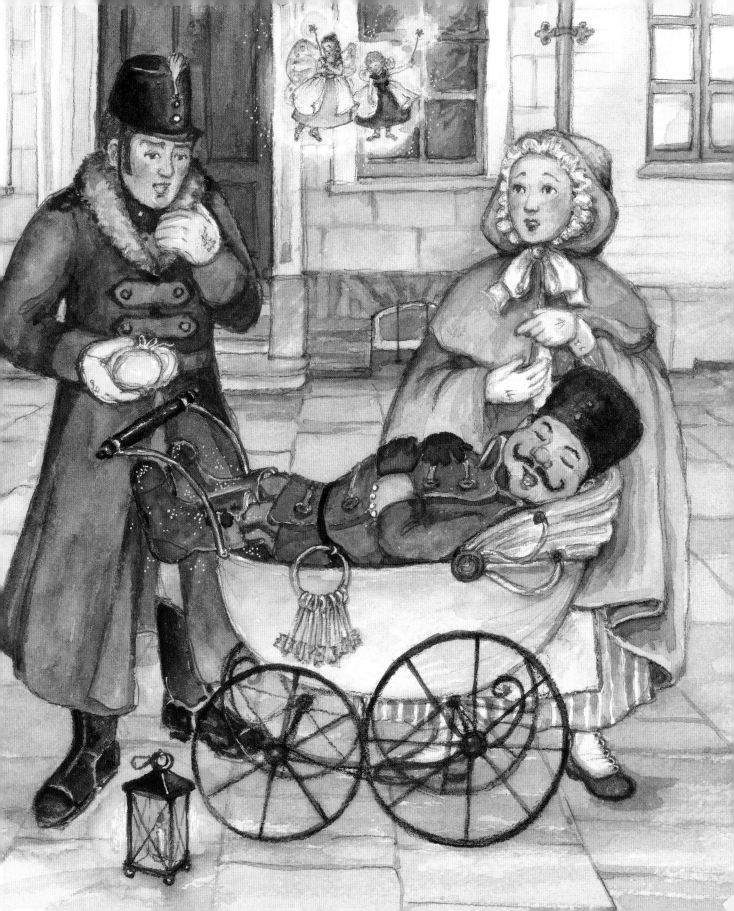

"It looks like the night watchman," the captain said
in amazement. "But how did he become a baby?"

The watchman snored even louder. As he tried to
turn over in his sleep, he kicked the boots off. Instantly
the watchman was back sitting on the bench, and he
was his normal size. The carriage was gone.

"Good evening, captain," the watchman said,
embarrassed to be caught napping. "Evening, Miss.
Just closing my eyes for a spell."

"Er, that's quite all right," said the stunned captain. "Say, why don't you go home to your wife and family and have a proper rest? I'll take over your watch."

"Why, thank you, sir," the watchman answered, surprised. "I am tuckered out. Why, I could sleep like a—"

Before the watchman could say "baby," the captain put the snack into the watchman's hand. The watchman rose slowly and left.

"What just happened?" asked the lady.

"I don't know," said the captain, shaking his head. "I'm as confused as you are. But it's late. You should be getting home to your own family."

"I don't have a family," she replied. "Not yet. I'm a nurse at the hospital. I was on my way to work." She looked at his kind face. "I don't have to be on duty for a while. Perhaps I could keep you company while you watch."

So the captain and the lady sat on the bench and talked and talked. Too soon it was time for her to go. The captain watched her walk away. He thought about his lonely life in his big house. He thought about how much he would like to have a wife and family, like the watchman.

"I wish I could see her again," he said out loud.

When she heard the word "wish," Lucky flew toward the boots.

Careful watched her quietly.

But then Lucky stopped. "Dr. Knapp and the watchman didn't *really* want what they wished for," Lucky said slowly. "That was wishful thinking. It was a mistake to try to make those wishes come true. But the captain *does* want what he's wishing for."

"That's right," Careful said. "And sometimes people need a little fairy dust to make their wishes come true. And sometimes they don't."

As the fairies watched, the captain rushed after the lady, calling her name. She turned back, beaming.

Careful touched Lucky's tiny wings with her wand. They grew into the big, beautiful wings of a true fairy. "You learned from your mistakes," she said. "And that is a most important lesson for every fairy.

Famous Fables, Lasting Virtues Tips for Parents

Now that you've read The Lucky Boots, *use these pages as a guide to teach your child the virtues in the story. By talking about the story and its message and engaging in the suggested activities, you can help your child develop good judgment and a strong moral character.*

About Learning from Mistakes

Everyone makes mistakes—children and grown-ups alike. In fact, child development experts agree that it is important for a child to experience making mistakes. Children who think their choices and actions must always be perfect have difficulty developing self-reliance, resiliency, or sufficient self-confidence. Teaching your child how to learn from her mistakes is one of the most valuable life lessons a parent can impart.

1. *Turn a mistake into an opportunity.* Show a positive attitude about your own mistakes as well as those of your child. Suppose you forgot to buy two key ingredients you needed for dinner. Discuss the problem with your child and figure out an alternate dish. Child development experts point out that the Chinese use the same word for *crisis* as they do for *opportunity.* Treat mistakes as opportunities to find new solutions.

2. *Avoid criticizing your child when a mistake occurs.* Suppose your child accidentally rips a picture she is drawing because she is coloring too hard. Don't say, "Now look what you've done. You're always so rough!" Instead, explain what happened in terms of the paper rather than the child—paper tears when too much force is applied. Then help your child tape or glue the paper together or give her a new piece of paper.

3. *Be supportive.* Different children react differently when they realize they have made a mistake. Some get frustrated, others get angry or embarrassed. Still others blame someone else or the circumstances. Listen to your child and be patient. Tell her you're proud of her efforts and encourage her to try again!

4. *Praise.* Be sure to praise your child when she applies the knowledge gained from making a mistake.